Papuan Warrior

This warrior, with his brightly painted face, comes from Papua New Guinea, a chain of islands north of Australia. He lives high up in the hills, where he farms and hunts. His headdress is made of the feathers of forest birds.

Clown

This circus clown loves to joke and make children laugh. Each clown's makeup is different. Clowning is a very old profession. Even before there were circuses, kings and lords had clowns to entertain their friends.

Egyptian Princess

This princess—daughter of the pharaoh, or king—comes from ancient Egypt. Her crown is made of gold and precious stones. She has made up her eyes so they look bigger, and she wears a black wig to keep the hot sun off her neck.

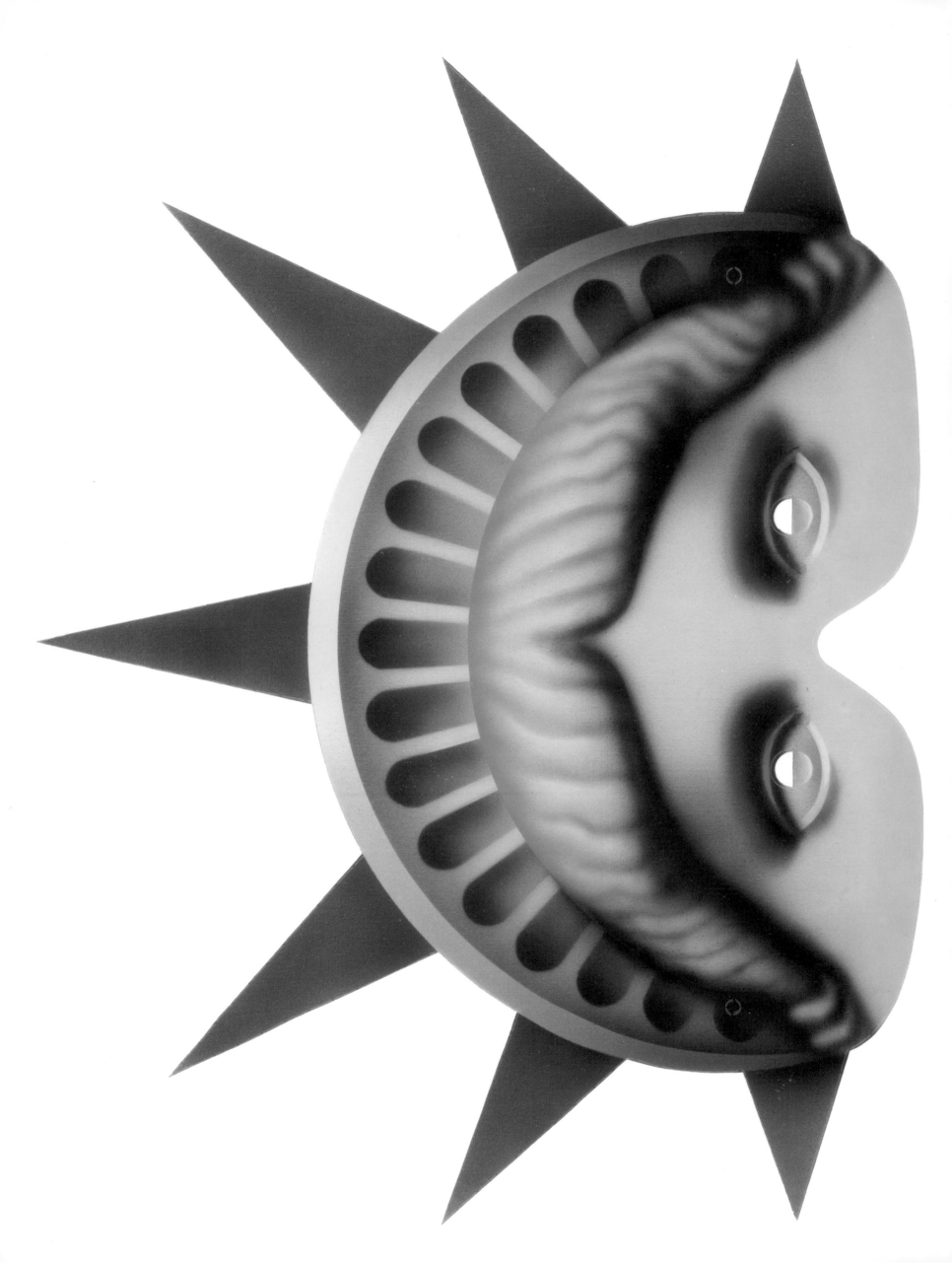

Statue of Liberty

Dedicated in 1886, the Statue of Liberty was a gift from France to the United States. Her nose is $4\frac{1}{2}$ feet long, and each eye measures $2\frac{1}{2}$ feet across. Over 151 feet tall from torch to toe, she stands in New York Harbor, welcoming immigrants to America and a new life.

Harvesttime Mask

This face is based on a design by Giuseppe Arcimboldo, a sixteenth-century Italian artist. Arcimboldo's best-known works are *The Four Seasons*, four paintings of faces made up of fruits and vegetables from the different seasons of the year.

Queen

Mary I was the first queen to reign in England. The daughter of Henry VIII, she inherited the throne after her father and brother died. She ruled from 1553 until 1558. There have been five queens of England since Mary.

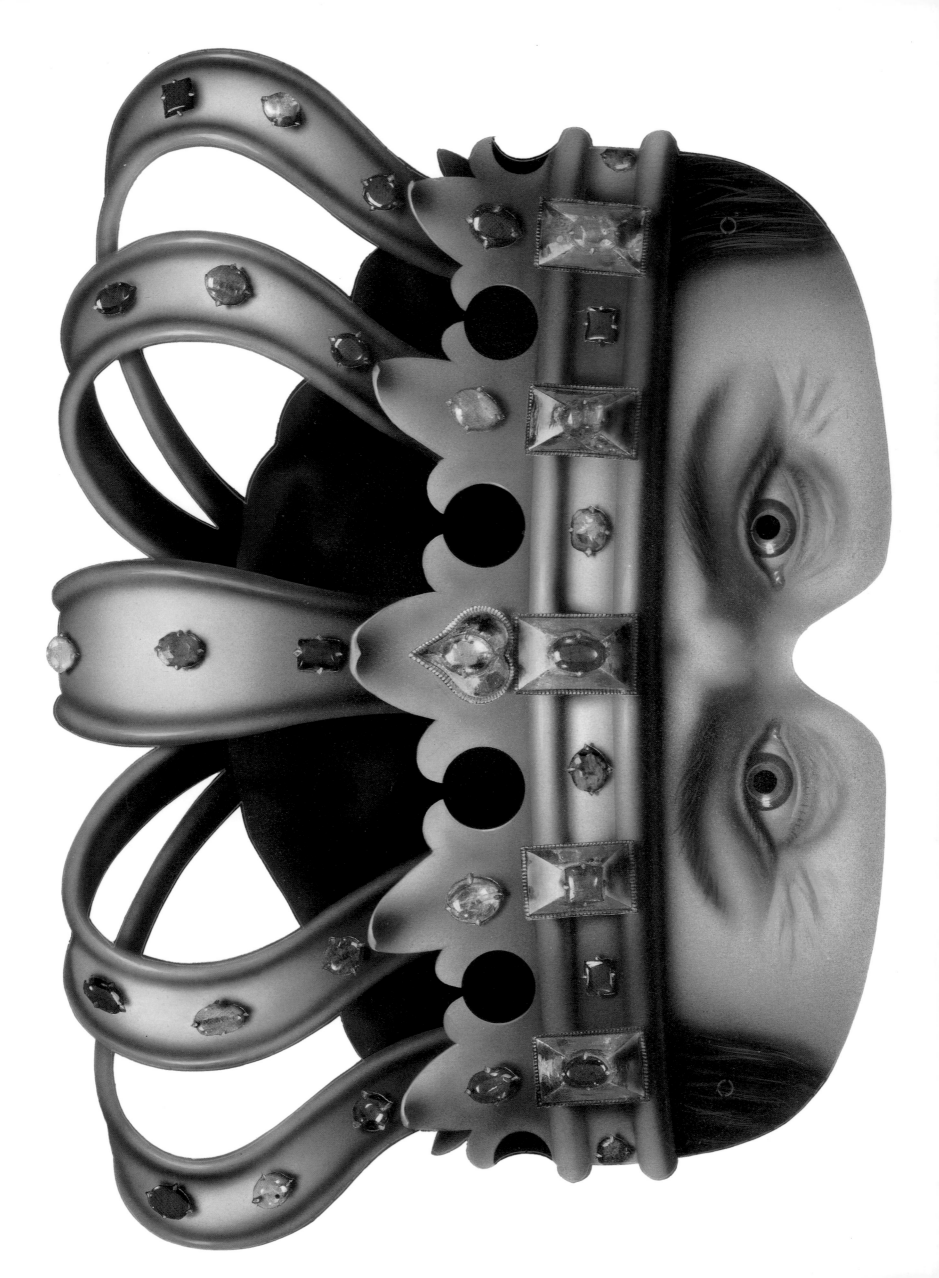

King

Alfred the Great was the first king of England. He lived from 849 to 899. Alfred was a brave soldier who fought the Vikings many times. He encouraged his people to learn to read and write, and even translated Latin books into Anglo-Saxon himself.

Fairy

People have always believed in fairies and fairy tales. Sometimes the fairies in stories are gentle and kind, and perform good magic. Sometimes they are mischievous, and sometimes they can be evil. Which kind of fairy do you think this is?

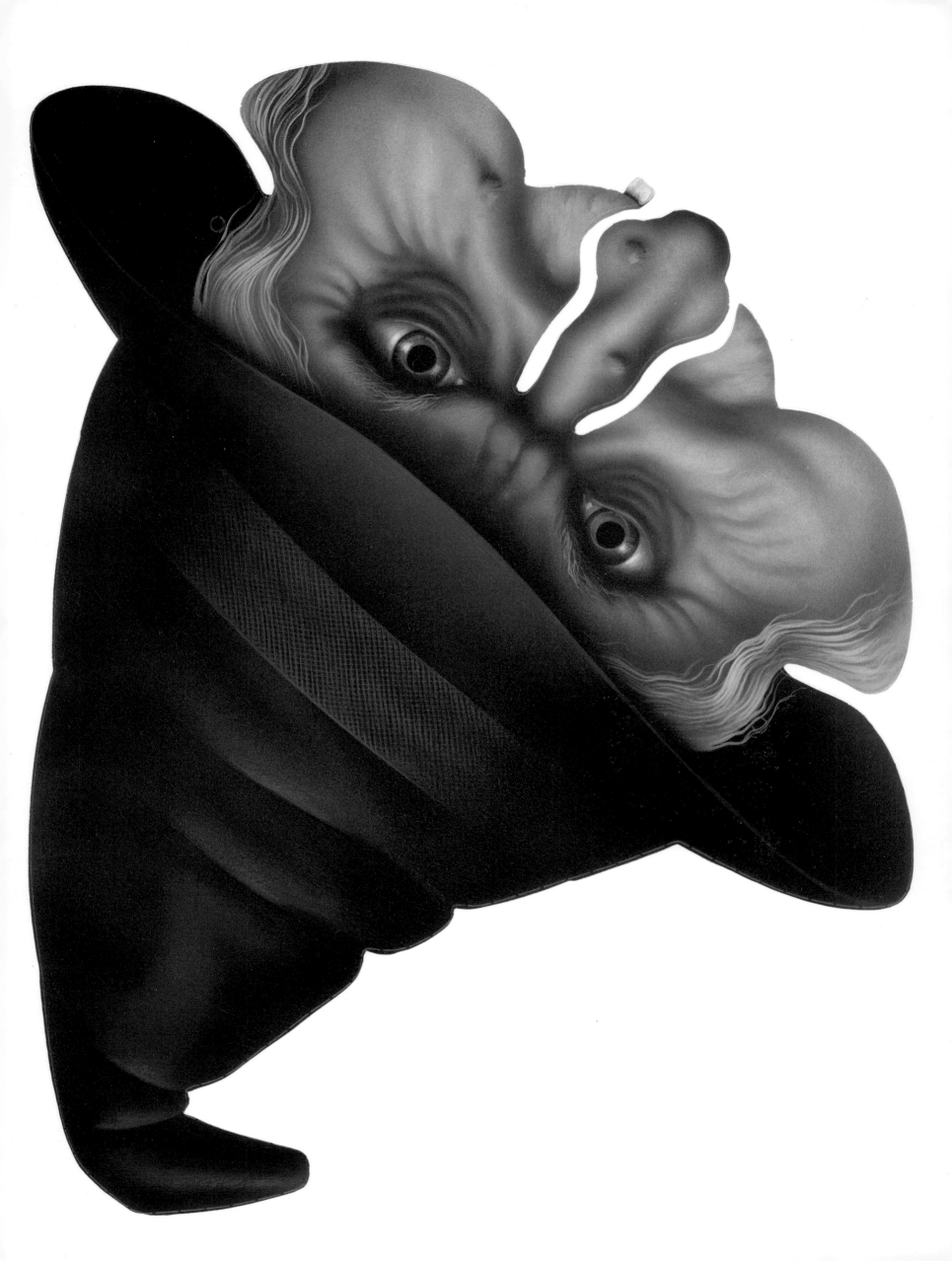

Witch

Long ago, many people believed in witches. Today we still like to hear and tell spooky stories about them. Halloween is supposed to be the witches' special night—a time for them to fly on their brooms, making magic and mischief.

Robot

Robots are machines that can do many different kinds of jobs. Imagine owning a special house-robot like this. Maybe it could dial the telephone, set the table, or even clean your room!

Pirate

In the eighteenth century, pirates sailed the high seas. They would prey on sailing ships that carried cargoes of gold and silver. Pirate ships flew the Jolly Roger—a black flag with a skull and crossbones—to scare their enemies.

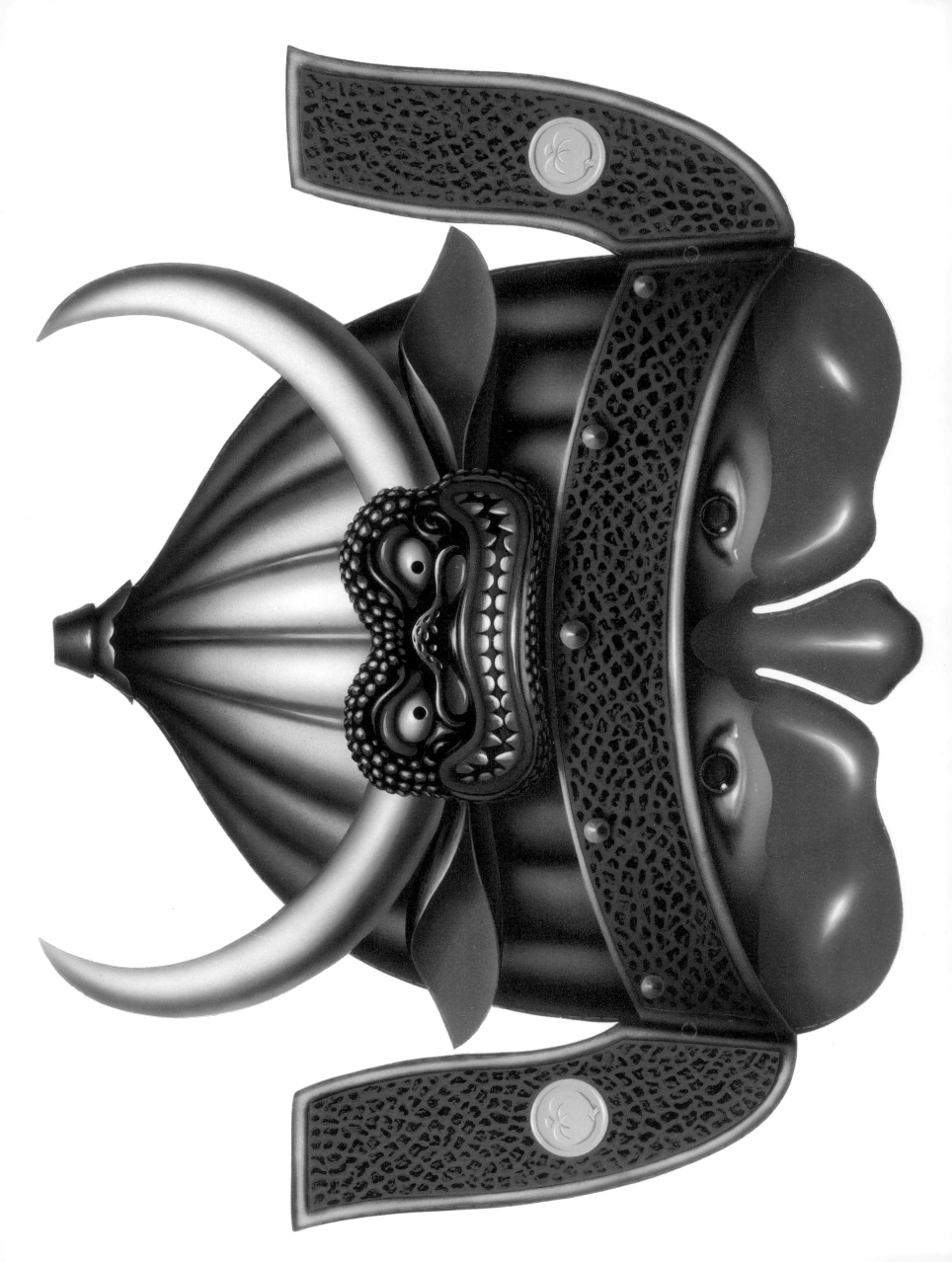

Samurai

This samurai warrior comes from ancient times when warlords ruled Japan. His armor is not only for protection but also to make him look fierce and to frighten his enemies. This warrior has two long swords for weapons.

Native American Chief

Years ago, many Native American tribes roamed the plains of the western United States. Only a chief or a brave warrior would wear a headdress like this, made from buffalo skin, buffalo horns, and eagle feathers. The Plains Indians believed that a war bonnet provided protection to its wearer in battle.

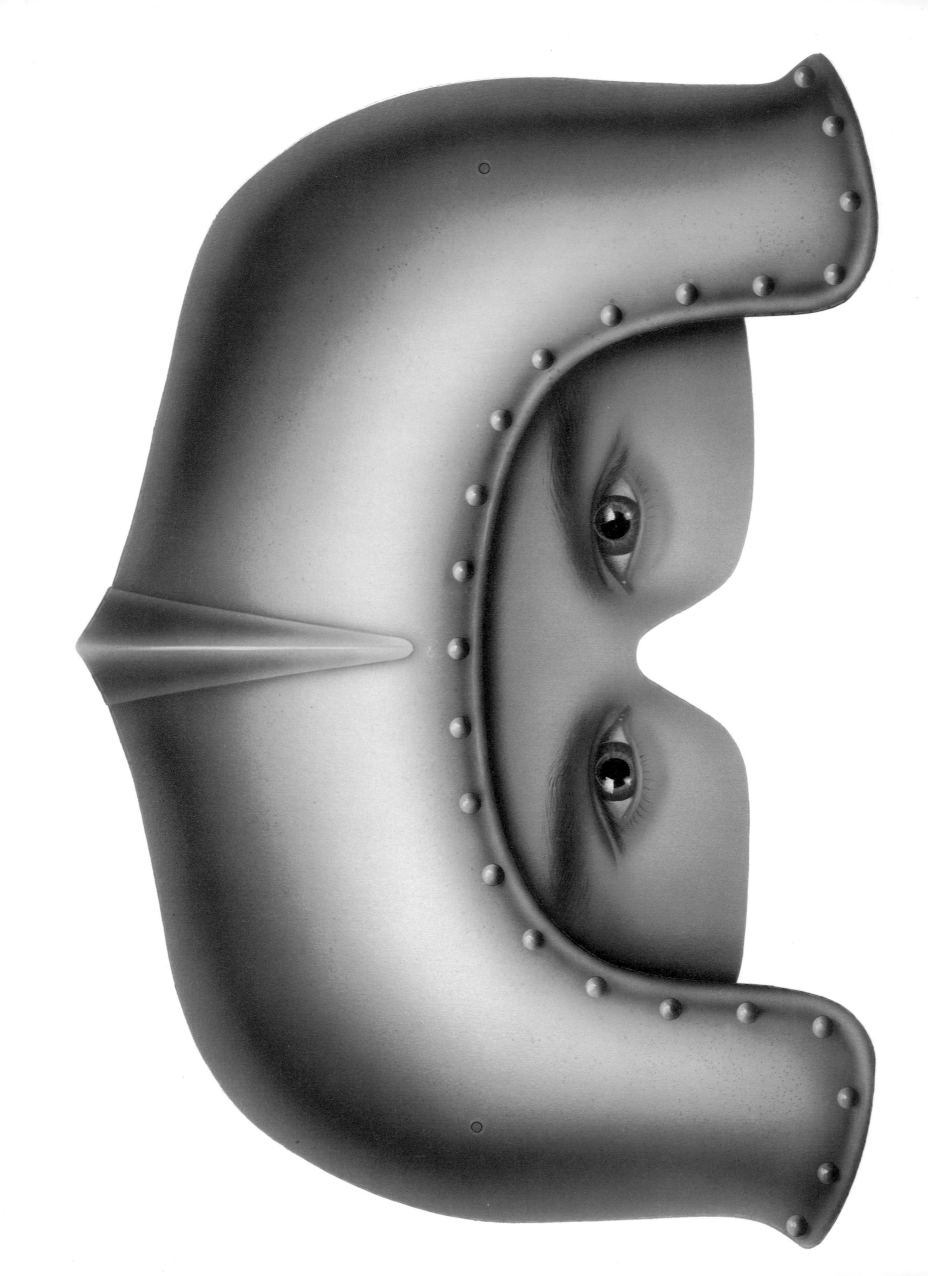

Medieval Knight

In the Middle Ages, knights covered themselves in armor from head to toe, for protection from arrows, swords, and axes. The armor was so heavy that the knights had to be helped onto their horses' backs. If they fell, often they could not get up again.

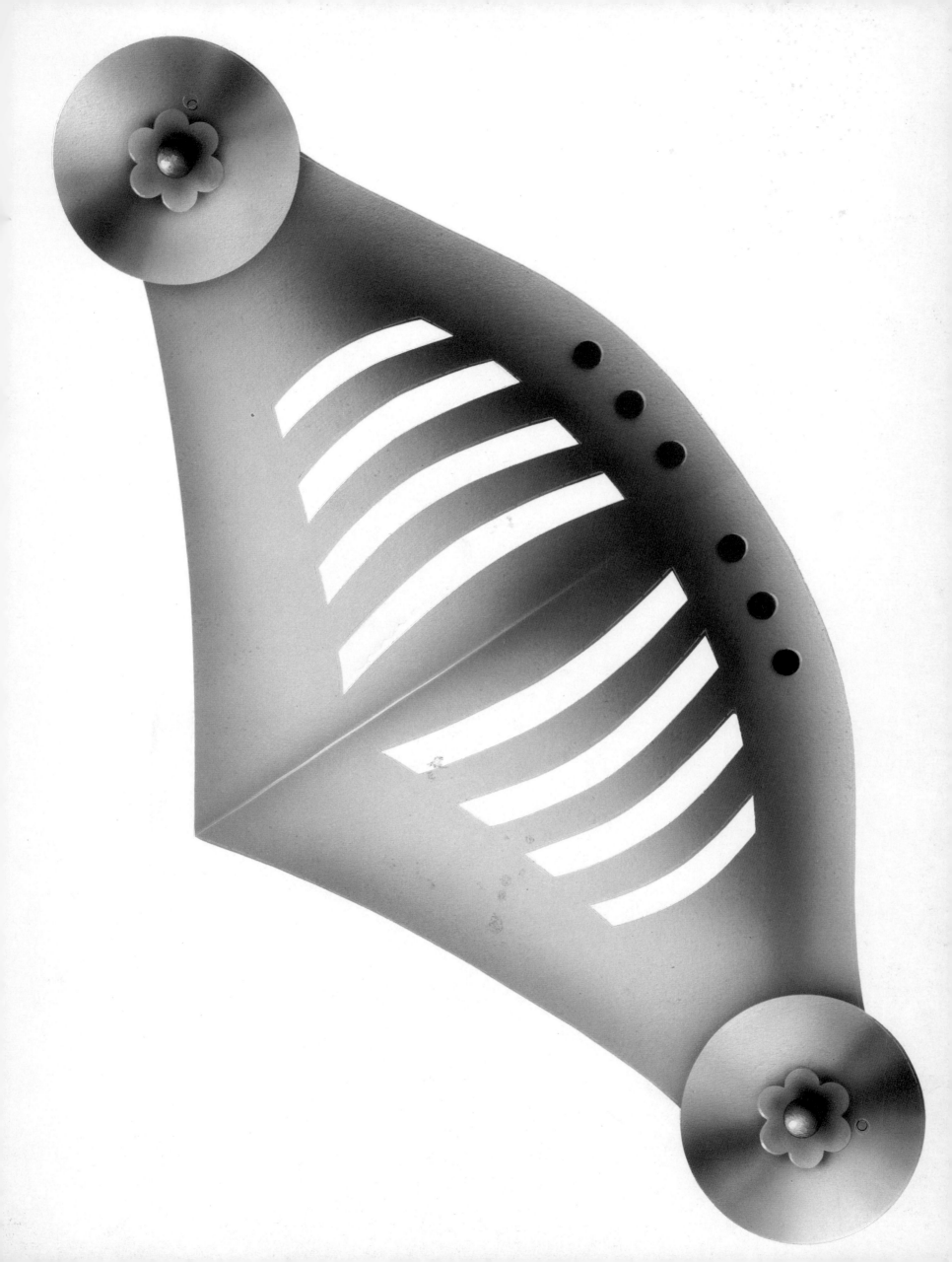

Visor

A visor, the front part of a knight's helmet, swung down on hinges to protect the face. The visor had holes to look and breathe through. It was very stuffy inside the helmet, and it was hard to see out clearly. But wearing it was better than being struck in the face during battle!

Copyright © 1988 by Éditions Gallimard
Based on English text by Sarah Matthews
English text © 1988 by Moonlight Publishing Ltd
Reissued 1996   All rights reserved.
Published in the United States 1996 by Dutton Children's Books,
a division of Penguin Books USA Inc.
375 Hudson Street, New York, New York 10014
Originally published in France 1988 by Éditions Gallimard
ISBN: 0-525-44544-7
Printed in Hong Kong
First Reissued Edition   10 9 8 7 6 5 4 3 2 1